D0236886

Bob's
Sporting Team

Book and DVD

Bob's Sporting Team

3
Wendy's
Big Match

33
One Shot Wendy

19
Bob on the Run

49
Eskimo Bob

Wendy's Big Match

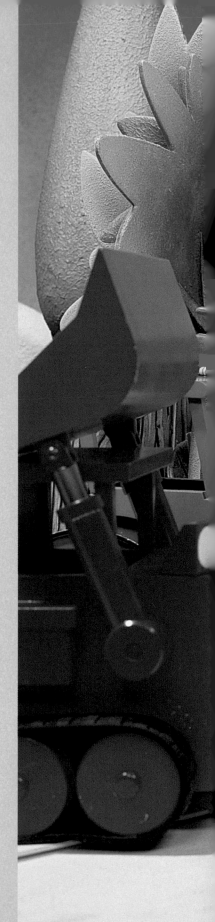

One bright sunny morning, Bob was reading in the yard.

"What's that?" Dizzy asked excitedly.

"It's a flower catalogue," Bob replied. "I'm ordering some flowers because I've entered us in the Brightest Building Yard Competition."

"But the yard's a mess!" cried Muck.

Bob nodded. "We're going to have a big tidy up before the judges arrive!"

"When are they coming?" asked Roley.

"At five o'clock," replied Bob.

"You'd better get started then," called Wendy, as she walked into the yard. "Muck can help you, Bob. The rest of the machines can come with me – we've got to get the football pitch ready today."

As Wendy jumped aboard Scoop, Bob popped Dizzy's football on top of her mixer.

"Have fun!" Bob called after them.

"Can we build it?" yelled Wendy, as they roared out of the yard.

"Yes, we can!" cried the machines.

When Wendy and the machines got to the football field, Dizzy started to run around after her ball.

"Brilliant! A proper pitch right here!" she squealed as she booted the football.

"Mind out, Dizzy," rumbled Roley. "I need to get this grass as flat as I can. If I leave any bumps, the ball will bounce all over the place."

Scoop unloaded the white paint and Wendy filled up the line-marking machine.

"What a team!" said Wendy proudly.

Wendy, Roley and Scoop were busy sorting out the football pitch. Dizzy was bored and wanted to play football.

Spud popped up from behind a bush.

"I'll play football with you, Dizzy," he said as he gave the ball a huge **Kick!** It flew high into the sky, then dropped slowly down to the ground.

Wendy looked up and saw it heading straight for her. Dragging the line-marking machine she ducked sideways, and the ball just missed her.

"Er, Wendy," gulped Scoop. "Look what you've done!"

Back at the yard, Bob was very busy cleaning up.

"Miaow!" grumbled Pilchard as Bob stepped over her.

"Oh, Pilchard!" cried Bob. "Find somewhere else to sleep!" Pilchard stalked off in a big sulk. She found a warm, sunny spot on top of the pile of rubbish that Bob had just swept up!

Muck came roaring back into the yard with his front dumper full of plants and flowers.

"Well done, Muck," said Bob. "Let's get those plants unloaded. Then we can start clearing away that pile of rubbish."

While Bob arranged his flowerpots, Muck busily scooped up all the building rubbish in his back dumper. He had no idea that Pilchard was fast asleep on the rubbish heap.

"Mi-aa-oo-w!" she howled crossly.

Bob turned around when he heard Pilchard's loud cries.

"Oh, no! Muck, STOP!" he yelled, as Muck thundered out of the yard with Pilchard wailing on top of his loaded dumper!

Muck slammed on his brakes and whizzed sharply around, sending rubbish flying all over the yard.

"What's the prob, Bob?"

"You've scooped up Pilchard with the rubbish!" cried Bob.

"Sorry," gulped Muck. "I didn't realise you were up there, Pilchard."

"Don't worry. We'll have to pick up all this rubbish!" sighed Bob, as Bird landed on his flowers.

"Bird! You're squashing my flowers! I don't think I'll ever have the yard clean and tidy by five o'clock!"

Wendy was making good progress on the football pitch. Lofty had lifted the goal posts into position. Roley had flattened the pitch perfectly. Scoop had helped Wendy to build the grandstand. Spud had cleaned up the wiggly white line.

"Oh, Wendy," squeaked Dizzy. "Please can we play a game of football, now?"

"I think we've got time," said Wendy checking her watch. "We're not due back at the yard until five o'clock."

"Yippeee!" shrieked Dizzy as she raced down the field after the ball.

Wendy blew her whistle to start the big match. Dizzy kicked off. And when Lofty got the ball, Dizzy nipped in and sent it up the field to Spud. Spud trapped the ball and headed it over to Wendy. Wendy dribbled the ball towards the open goalmouth and Wham! She booted it in.

"What a goal!" yelled Dizzy. "Hooray for Wendy!"

"Oh, that was fun!" gasped Wendy. "But we must get back to the yard," she said.

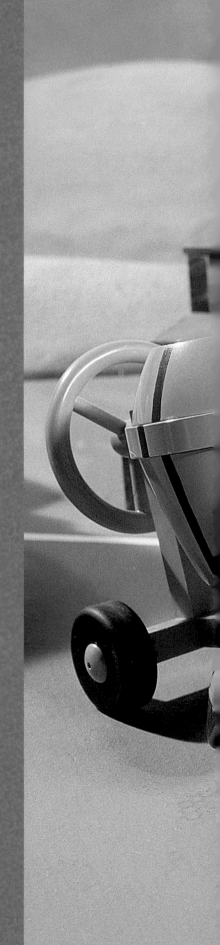

Bob had finished tidying the yard. It looked bright and clean, but Bob's face and overalls were covered in dirt!

"I'd better go and smarten myself up before the judges arrive," he said to Muck.

Suddenly they heard a car draw up outside the yard.

"I think we've got visitors," said Muck.

"Oh, no!" gasped Bob. "The judges are early!"

When Wendy and the machines arrived back at the yard, they were amazed at how smart and tidy it looked.

"It's really, really pretty!" squeaked Dizzy.

"You've done a great job, Bob," said Wendy. "What did the judges say?"

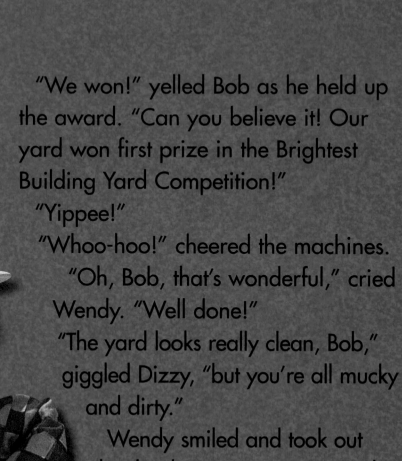

"We won!" yelled Bob as he held up the award. "Can you believe it! Our yard won first prize in the Brightest Building Yard Competition!"

"Yippee!"

"Whoo-hoo!" cheered the machines.

"Oh, Bob, that's wonderful," cried Wendy. "Well done!"

"The yard looks really clean, Bob," giggled Dizzy, "but you're all mucky and dirty."

Wendy smiled and took out her hanky to wipe some smudgy marks off Bob's face.

"Lucky for you it wasn't the Brightest Builder competition," she teased.

"You're right there, Wendy!" laughed Bob.

THE END

Bob on the Run

One morning Wendy was explaining to the team about the job they had to do that day.

"The sports pavilion is getting old and it needs knocking down," she said.

Bob came jogging into the yard.

"Oh hello, Bob. You're looking very sporty!" said Wendy.

"I'm doing a sponsored run this afternoon," Bob panted. "I'm raising money to build a new sports pavilion."

"What's a sponsored run, Bob?" asked Muck.

"Well, I'll go on a run, and people sponsor me by giving me some money for every mile I run," explained Bob.

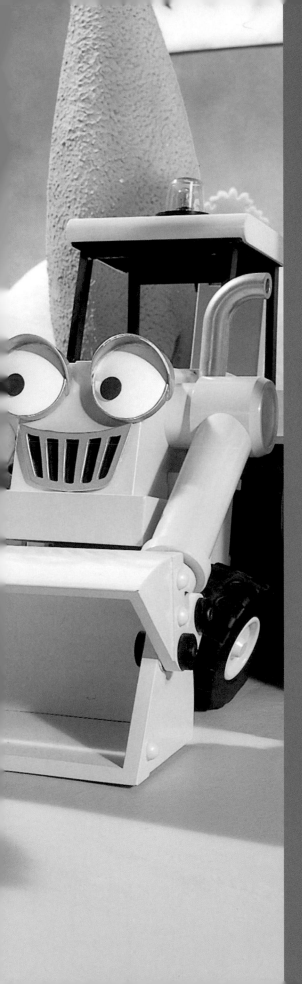

"Good luck, Bob. All right everyone. Let's go!" Wendy called to the team.

When the team arrived at the old sports pavilion, Mrs Percival was there, painting a red line on a picture of a giant thermometer.

"Hello, Mrs Percival. What are you doing?" asked Scoop.

"The red line on this picture shows how much money we have raised so far for the new sports pavilion," said Mrs Percival. "We're not on target yet."

"So you need to raise more money?" asked Scoop.

"Yes," replied Mrs Percival.

"I've got an idea! While Bob's doing his sponsored run, we could get people to sponsor us to demolish this old pavilion," cried Scoop.

"What a good idea, Scoop," cried Wendy. "Dizzy! Muck! Please can you go with Mrs Percival and get sponsors for us to demolish the old pavilion."

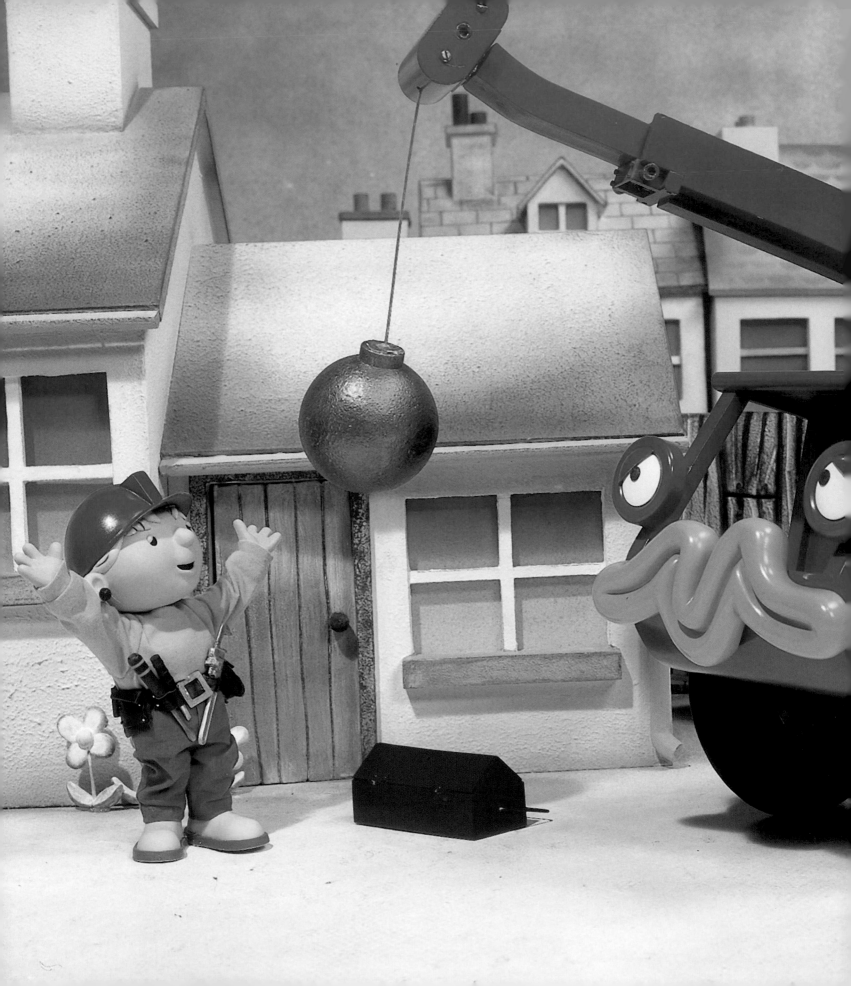

Back at the yard, later that day…
"Right, team. Let's go! We've got a building to demolish!" said Wendy, as she finished attaching Lofty's wrecking ball.

At the same time, in a field, Mrs Percival was starting the sponsored run.
"On your marks, Bob, get set, go!" cried Mrs Percival.
Bob set off on his run. Back at the old pavilion, Roley rolled into the wall with a THUMP and sent the bricks tumbling. Lofty had got the hang of his wrecking ball and was bashing big holes out of the wall.
BANG, CRASH!

The machines were enjoying knocking down the pavilion. Scoop was shovelling tiles from the roof with his back scoop, when suddenly, Lofty swung his wrecking ball too quickly and the cable got tangled around a nearby rugby goal post.

"Ohh! Help!" cried Lofty. "I'm stuck!"

"Oh, Lofty! We'll never get you untangled! Scoop, can you hold the wrecking ball, while I try to take it off," said Wendy. "I'll just get my special spanner… oh, no, I gave it to Bob earlier," cried Wendy. "How am I going to find Bob now? He'll be doing his run."

"I know, Wendy," said Roley. "We can send Bird to find Bob! He'll be quick."

"Thank you, Bird," said Wendy, as Bird flew off to find Bob.

"Meep!" chirped Bird, when he saw Bob.

"Oh, hello Bird," panted Bob. "Not far to run now! Is something wrong?"

"Meep!" cried Bird, even louder this time.

"You want me to follow you?" asked Bob.

"Meep!" cried Bird.

"OK then. Lead on!"

A little later, Bob and Bird arrived at the demolition site. Bob was worn out from running.

"What seems to be the problem?" Bob panted.

"It's Lofty. He's got stuck!" explained Wendy.

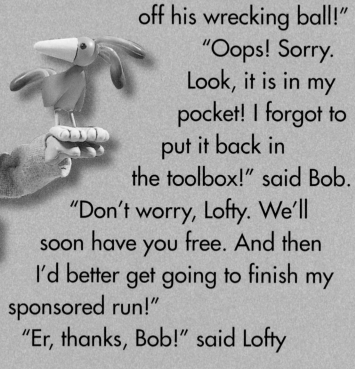

"You have the spanner we need to take off his wrecking ball!"

"Oops! Sorry. Look, it is in my pocket! I forgot to put it back in the toolbox!" said Bob.

"Don't worry, Lofty. We'll soon have you free. And then I'd better get going to finish my sponsored run!"

"Er, thanks, Bob!" said Lofty

"Well done, Bob!" cried Mrs Percival as Bob finally staggered across the finishing line a little later. "Where have you been? I thought you weren't going to make it."

"I had to sort out a little job on the way!" laughed Bob. "So I've had to run twice as far!"

"That's marvelous!" cried Mrs Percival. "Because you have run twice as far as you were meant to, that means you have raised twice as much sponsorship money!"

"Brilliant!" said Bob. "Let's go and see how the rest of the team have got on with the demolition."

The old pavilion was gone!

"Well done everyone!" said Mrs Percival. "With the money we've raised from Bob's run and the demolition, we've reached our target!"

"Right, so it looks like we will be back here again next week," said Bob.

"Er… why is that, Bob?" asked Lofty.

"To build the new sports pavilion, of course!" laughed Bob.
And everyone cheered!

THE END

One Shot Wendy

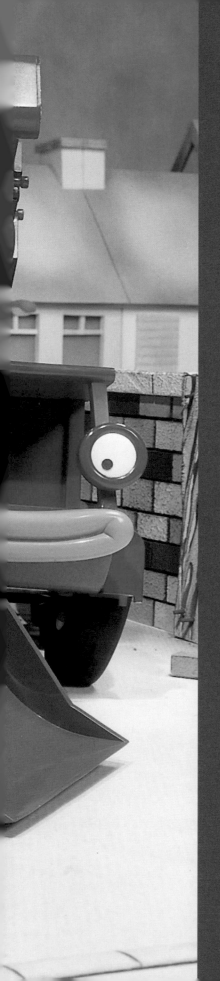

What's all this funny stuff for?" asked Dizzy, as Lofty lowered a wooden clown's face into Muck's dumper.

"We're going to build a crazy golf course today," said Bob. "And I'm going to build a special surprise for the final hole!"

"What's a crazy golf course?" asked Dizzy.

"It's a golf course where you hit the balls through all sorts of crazy obstacles – like this clown's face!" explained Bob.

"Can we build it?" Wendy asked.

"Yes, we can!" everyone replied.

"Come on everyone!" Wendy called as she jumped onto Muck's step. Dizzy, Lofty and Scoop followed them out of the yard.

"Oh dear!" said Wendy when she got to the first hole. "I've still got the instructions. Bob will need these to help him put together his special surprise at the last hole! I'd better phone him."

Bob had just unpacked the bits for the final hole when his phone rang.

"Hello, Wendy. You've got the instructions? Oh, don't worry about that, I don't need them. Instructions are for people who don't know what they're doing! Bye!" he chuckled.

Bob picked up a piece of wood. "Umm… I wonder where this piece goes?"

Back at the first hole, Dizzy was helping Wendy. Scoop had dug out an area in the grass and she filled it with wet cement.

"Now, can you roll through the cement, please, Dizzy," Wendy said.

"But it's still wet," giggled Dizzy.

"Your tracks will be perfect for the ball to run down," Wendy explained.

Dizzy took a big run up and whizzed through the cement.

"Wheee!" she shouted as cement flew out everywhere.

Bob was just finishing the surprise for the final hole. It was a wooden windmill! It had a little hole for the ball at the bottom and sails that went round at the top.

"Nearly there! Just got to fix this roof in place," said Bob as he climbed inside the windmill to nail the roof on. "We didn't need instructions, did we Pilchard?"

"Miaow!" Pilchard cried, looking at Bob in a funny way. It had taken Bob a lot longer than it should have done to put the windmill together!

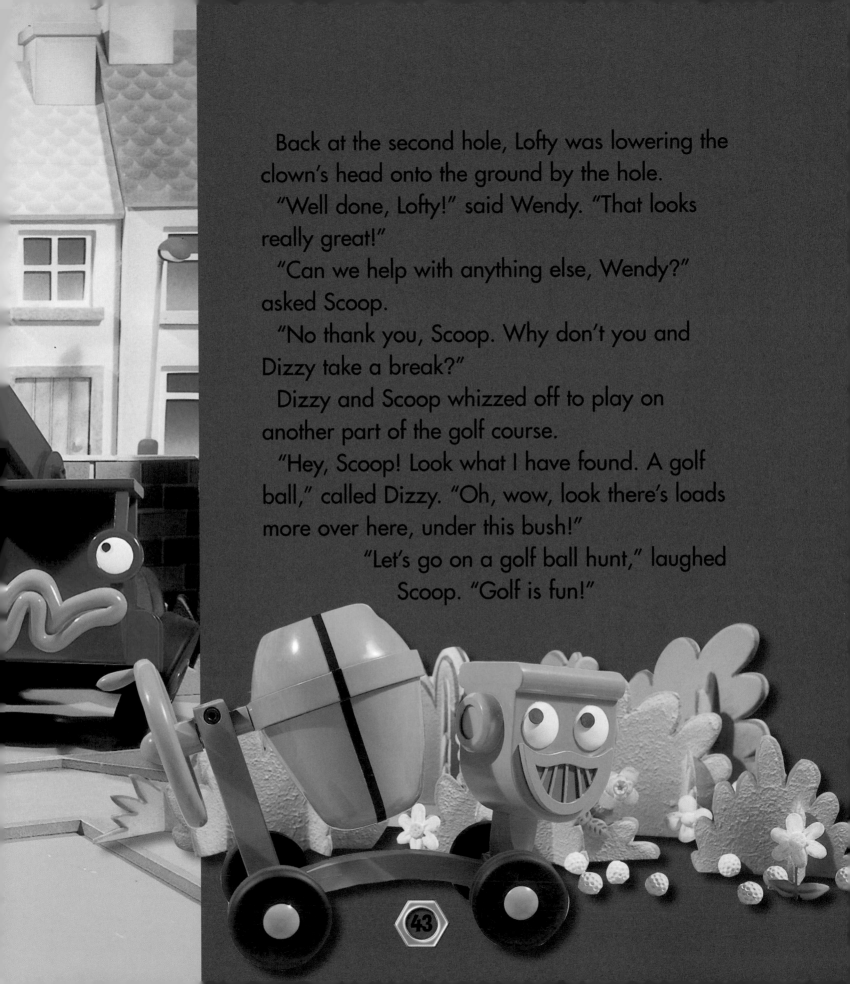

Back at the second hole, Lofty was lowering the clown's head onto the ground by the hole.

"Well done, Lofty!" said Wendy. "That looks really great!"

"Can we help with anything else, Wendy?" asked Scoop.

"No thank you, Scoop. Why don't you and Dizzy take a break?"

Dizzy and Scoop whizzed off to play on another part of the golf course.

"Hey, Scoop! Look what I have found. A golf ball," called Dizzy. "Oh, wow, look there's loads more over here, under this bush!"

"Let's go on a golf ball hunt," laughed Scoop. "Golf is fun!"

Back at the third hole, Muck, Lofty and Wendy were just finishing putting the target obstacle in place.

"I'll ring Bob to see how he is getting on with his surprise," said Wendy and she called Bob on her mobile phone.

"He's nearly finished it. Come on Lofty, Muck, let's go," said Wendy, and they set off to the yard to collect Bob's surprise.

"Wow!" said Muck when he saw the windmill.

"Er, where's Bob?" asked Lofty.

Lofty carefully hooked the top of the windmill and got ready to move it. When the lid came up they found Bob. He'd been stuck inside!

"Ha, ha! How did you get in there?" laughed Muck.

"Um, I don't really know," muttered Bob.

"So you didn't need those instructions, then, Bob…?" laughed Wendy.

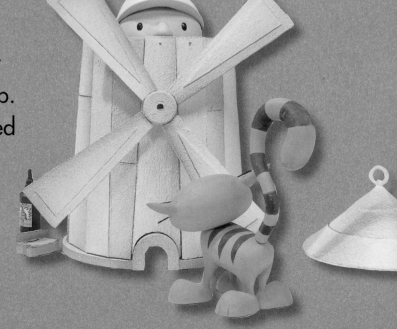

The team set off to the final hole on the crazy golf course.

"Yippee! A windmill!" called Dizzy as she arrived with Scoop and lots of golf balls.

"OK! You can put the windmill in place now," Bob said to Lofty.

"Ohh, look!" cried Dizzy as the sails began to move round and round.

"Let's have a game to check everything works properly," Bob suggested. He lined up in front of the clown's face and took a swing at the ball. It bounced around and landed right back in front of him.

Bob tried again. This time the ball dropped right into the clown's mouth.

"Great shot, Bob!" said Scoop.

"This hole looks easier!" said Bob as he took a big swing at the ball.

It flew up off the concrete, completely missed the target and nearly hit Bird.

"Toot! Toot!" screeched Bird.

"Ooops! Sorry, Bird!" said Bob.

"That was close," rumbled Roley.

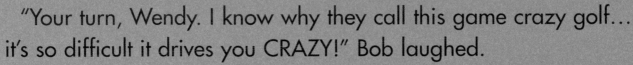

"Your turn, Wendy. I know why they call this game crazy golf...
it's so difficult it drives you CRAZY!" Bob laughed.

Wendy lined up her shot. She swung her club back and hit the
ball straight into the hole in the target.

"Hooray!" everyone cheered.

"Great shot! Well done, Wendy!" said Bob.

"You got a hole in one!"

THE END

Eskimo Bob

Wendy and her sister had just got back from their skiing holiday.

"Did you have a good time?" asked Bob.

"We certainly did," said Wendy. "Skiing's really good fun."

"You ought to try it, Bob," said Jenny.

But Bob wasn't so sure. It looked tricky to him.

As Farmer Pickles made his way back to the farmhouse that evening, he noticed part of the roof needed repairing.

"I meant to ask Bob to check on that roof," he said to Scruffty. "Oh, well. It's too late to do anything tonight."

But during the night it began to snow. By morning, Bobsville was completely covered. Bob, Muck and Scoop set out early to grit the roads.

Later that morning, when Bob had returned to the yard to get ready for the rest of the day's jobs, Mr Bentley called and asked if Bob could clear a snowdrift outside the town.

"No problem, Mr Bentley!" said Bob.

As Bob and the machines were getting ready to go out again, Jenny and Wendy came into the yard.

"Bob! Why on earth have you got tennis rackets on your feet?" asked Jenny.

"They're my snowshoes, Jenny. Like the Eskimos wear to get around on the snow."

Jenny laughed. "I still think you ought to try the skis. They'd be a lot easier."

Just after Bob left, Farmer Pickles rang the office. His roof was sagging even more with the snow on it.

"Bob's out on a job, Farmer Pickles," said Wendy. "I'll come over and take a look if you like." Then she remembered something. "Oh, no! We don't have Scoop and his snowplough!"

"You don't need a snowplough," Jenny told her. "I've got a better idea."

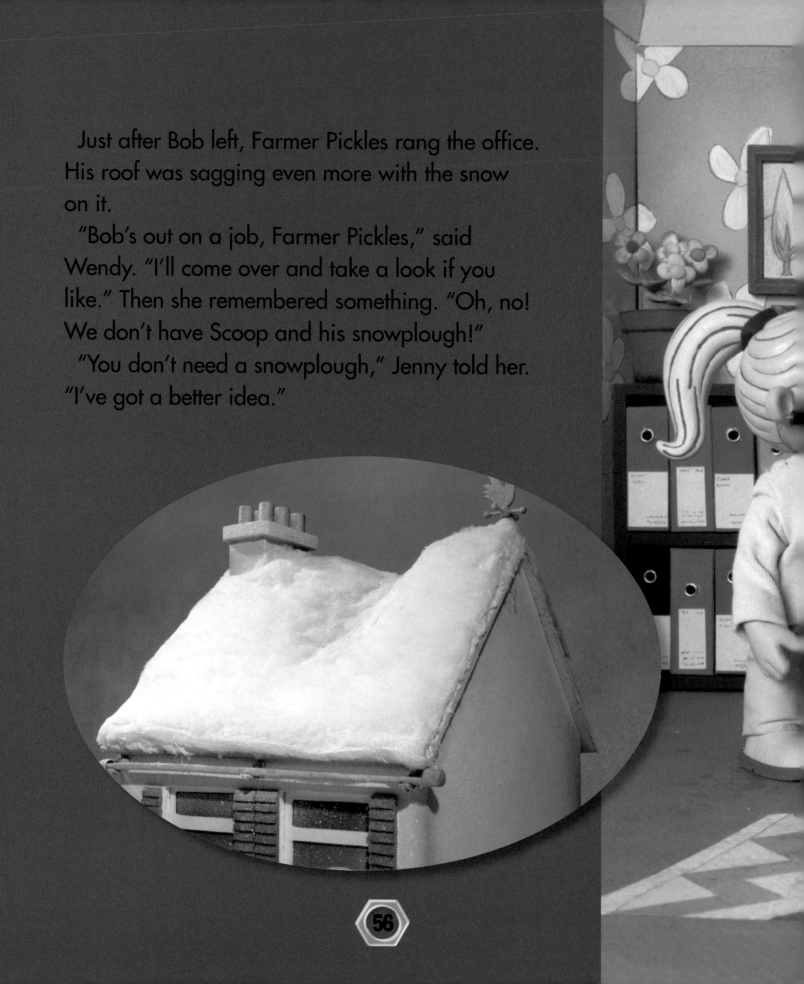

Wendy and Jenny reached the farm on their skiis in no time.
Wendy saw immediately what was needed for the roof and rang
Bob on his mobile. He had just finished the job for Mr Bentley.

"Hello, Wendy… yes we have battens at the yard… yes, I'll pick
them up and bring Lofty. I'm on my way!"

"Come in out of the cold and snow, while we wait for Bob," said
Farmer Pickles to Wendy and Jenny.

In the farmyard, Spud saw Wendy and Jenny's skiis stuck in the snow.

"Ooh! These look fun!" he laughed as he tried a pair on. As he tried to move forwards, he slipped and suddenly he was flying through the air. Crash! Spud landed with a thump on Scruffty's kennel.

"What happened?" shouted Wendy, as she, Jenny and Farmer Pickles rushed outside.

Poor Scruffty's kennel was a mess.

"Sorry, Farmer Pickles," Spud groaned. "It was an accident."

"Don't worry," said Jenny. "Leave it to me!"

When Bob arrived he and the team quickly repaired Farmer Pickles' roof.

"Great job, Bob!" said Farmer Pickles. "It looks as good as new!"

"Yoo, hoo!" called Jenny. "Come and see what I've made!"

"Oh, wow, Jenny… you've made Scruffty an igloo!" said Wendy.

"Ruff, ruff!" barked Scruffty. He loved his new kennel.

"Right, everybody," said Bob. "I think our work is finished for today. Let's go home!"

"Why don't you borrow Wendy's skiis and ski home with me?" Jenny asked. "Scoop can take Wendy home."

"Well… OK, then. I suppose I could have a go," said Bob. He set off holding onto Lofty.

"This is fun!" laughed Bob. Then Lofty let go off him…

"Wooooohhh!" cried Bob as he wobbled and crashed, into a big snowdrift.

"Can I do it?" giggled Bob.

"Err… I don't think so!" laughed Lofty loudly.

THE END